MICHELLE'S LIFE IS A MESS!

I come away from the alcove with a sudden jolt—sending myself, the Shrink, and the fire extinguisher flying. That harmless looking, little red tank goes beserk—foam squizzles everywhere. Shrink leaps on it, but obviously isn't familiar with the latest fire-fighting techniques. All she manages to do is point the wild nozzle in my face.

By the time the extinguisher loses its zing, Shrink and I look like the Abominable Snowman's drippy cousins, just wandering in from an unfortunate expedition to the South Pole.

SCHOOLHOUSE NOVELS

Peanut Butter Is Forever

MELANIE ZOLA

SCHOOLHOUSE PRESS

Series Editor Meguido Zola

Illustrations Jock MacRae
Editors Elma Schemenauer, Peggy Foy
Design David Taylor/Taylor/Levkoe Associates
Typesetting Trigraph Inc.

Published in 1986 by
Schoolhouse Press, Inc.
4700 Rockside Road
Independence, Ohio 44131

ISBN 0-8086-0314-0

Library of Congress Cataloging-in-Publication Data

Zola, Melanie, 1952-
  Peanut butter is forever.

  (Schoolhouse novels)
  Summary: Michelle learns the true meaning of
friendship when she is asked to renounce her
unpopular friend before they enter junior high
school.
  [1. Friendship—Fiction 2. Schools—Fiction]
I. MacRae, Jock, ill. II. Title.
PZ7.Z723Pe 1986   [Fic]   85-27739
ISBN 0-8086-0314-0

86/87/88/89   5-4-3-2-1

Table of Contents

To my dear sister, Teresa McLeod; and to Angela Dereume, a peanut-butter kind of friend.

Chapter One

TEREZ HAS HER SAY

"WHAT d'you mean, I've got to quit being friends with Dora Klutzmann?" I yell at Terez. "Believe it or not, you're only my big sister—not my mother. I'll choose my *own* friends, thanks."

I've had it with Terez bugging me about Klutzy.

Terez flicks her long blonde bangs to the side—a very 'in' thing to do. I can nearly see the whites of her eyes.

"Look, Terez," I try to explain for the zillionth time. "You've never had a friend like Klutzy…"

"You betcha, Michelle," sneers Terez. "I wouldn't be caught dead going into seventh grade with a zero like her."

"Dora Klutzmann is NOT a zero. She's a better friend than you'll ever have," I shout, riled. "You don't have anyone who'll ride cardboard with you down the coulee hills..."

"Woe is me," yawns Terez. "Who's interested?"

"You didn't let me finish—it's not just that," I bluster. "Klutzy once spent a whole hour picking cactus thorns out of my rear after a hill scramble."

"That's precisely why I don't bother with the hills at the coulee—unless I'm riding with a guy who has a hot dirt bike," sniffs Terez. She flicks her bangs again, as if to alter the wave length of our conversation. "But that's all beside the point—take my advice and drop that Klutzmann drip before you move up into seventh grade."

"I told you: I don't want your advice. You never *listen* to me. You never hear what I'm saying about..."

"It's *you* who should start listening, Michelle. And don't get into a snit again. *I'm* taking time out of my full and satisfying life to help *you* clue in to some of the problems *you're* about to face in junior high..."

I roll my eyes. "You sound like the sex education teacher."

"I have your best interests at heart," Terez says primly, "or I wouldn't be bothering. Do I ever *not* put you first?"

"Only about 99 per cent of the time," I come back. "And the other one per cent that you *do* put me first is when you want to volunteer me to dry dishes."

Terez shrugs off my comment with a toss of her golden hair: "It's *your* life I'm trying to save."

Terez is buffing her latest heart-throb's ring on my bedspread as she talks. She examines it on her long, graceful fingers. Her bronzed coral nails match her manicured toes. Everything Terez says and does matches the 'in' crowd at Alexander Henry Senior High School.

And now that I'm going into seventh grade at Clearview Junior High, Terez is trying to palm off the 'in-crowd' gospel on me. Make me one of the chosen in junior high—the way she is at the senior high, just across the school yard.

"Save my life—oh, sure. And ruin Klutzy's. Thanks a bunch, but no thanks," I snap. "Klutzy is my best friend."

"Was," corrects Terez. "Think of her in the past tense."

"Tense is exactly how I'm feeling. So get lost," I yell.

Terez's azure eyeshadow flashes. "I'm warning you, Mitch. Your dog-faced friend is a real loser. A klutz. In more than just her nickname. She may have been all right in your hokey little elementary school, but you'll be *dead* if you hang around with her now that you're going into junior high. The kids will make you an outcast along with her in no time flat."

"So I'll wrap my body in rags and ring little bells before I come onto the school grounds."

I start hobbling and I grasp Terez's arm. "Lepers, lepers," I croak. "Money for the lepers."

I straighten up and look normal again. "Who knows? Maybe Klutzy and I will end up collecting a bundle and leave Lyndhurst as millionaires!"

Terez stands up, steaming. If only her boyfriend "Knox-Stinky-Sox" could see her now! His permed hair would frizz. This is *not* super-cool Terez, cheerleader sweetheart for the great Alexander Henry Sugar Kings basketball team. Poor old Knox would never believe this is the same Terez he goes steady with.

"You little jerk!" she shrieks at me. "You *deserve* what you'll get at school. Don't blame me if you're a social reject the rest of your life. You and your short-sighted, cross-eyed Dora Klutzmann. Just don't mention that you're any relation to *me*! If you so much as walk into that school yard with her, I'll refuse to admit you even exist!"

"You mean you'd ignore me?" I ask innocently.

"Exactly. Now you've got it."

"Hmm," I muse. "Sounds tempting."

Terez stomps to my bedroom door. Then, at the last moment, she turns for an exit line. It's not for nothing that my sister gets all the lead roles in the Drama Club productions.

"I know what Clearview Junior High is all about..." she sighs emphatically. "I have striven and overcome."

"What in the world is *that* supposed to mean?" I demand.

"What does striven and overcome mean?" Terez repeats, annoyed. She looks aghast. One of her best lines has been wasted on me. "It means, dough-head, that I've learned the game and I can play it with the best of them. And *you* can profit from any advice I give you."

"You don't say." I sound impressed. "But I guess they haven't taught you how to get your facts straight."

"What facts?" Terez whirls round. She's fallen for my bait. I see in her frown that she thinks I'm going to taunt her about the marks on her last report card.

I let her stew a moment. The one thing I have inherited along with Terez is a sense of dramatic timing. I pause and look down at my own poor chewed fingernails.

"You said that Dora Klutzmann is short-sighted and cross-eyed," I say finally. "The fact is that Klutzy's eyes are a perfect twenty-twenty. She...she just *sees* things a bit differently, that's all."

Terez sniffs and storms out the door. She has to change into her bikini—if you can call that changing into anything. She's got a pool party at Marsha Dumfl's to go to. Then they'll probably cruise Mayor Magrath Drive in Knox's convertible—with Terez at the wheel to show off her new driver's licence. That's Terez's idea of a big night out.

Me—I walk over to Klutzy's with the hot afternoon sun blazing on my back. The sizzling expanse of blue sky empties my head of nagging thoughts about Terez and the worries she's given me. So what if Klutzy and I never get popular? We never asked to leave sixth grade. Most of the kids in elementary school just ignored us and let us be each other's best friends. Why should junior high school be any different?

Anyway, all I want to think about now are these last golden days of August. Klutz and I'll probably go down to Geauga Lake Park and climb sky-high on the roller coaster. With any luck the loop will rattle us silly. We don't ask for much, just good times together. Terez and her type can go jump in an irrigation ditch, for all I care.

As far as I'm concerned, it'll always be just Klutzy and me. As far as I'm concerned, that's the last and final word.

Chapter Two

BIRDS OF A FEATHER

"OH, Michelle, love," Mama calls as she leaves the kitchen. "May I talk to you in your room for a minute? Terez will be glad to do the dishes for you."

Terez smirks. "My pleasure, Mitchy, dear. I believe Mother has summoned you..."

Terez is obviously up to no good. And she's got Mama working with her.

I sneer back as I leave the table, "Terez, you make me want to puke."

"I heard that, Miss," says Mama sternly. "It's quite uncalled for. Terez is only trying to help you."

Mama sits on my bed and pats a spot beside her. This 'Let's be buddies' stuff chokes me, 'cause I know it's part of Terez's 'Don't be buddies with Klutzy' campaign.

I close the door and sit down.

"Terez is trying to help me, sure," I say unconvinced. "And what do you call what she's trying to do to Klutzy? Dora didn't get her nickname for nothing, Mama. She's a klutz—you know that. She'll be *lost* in junior high without me as a friend."

Mama bulldozes ahead without even blinking at what I've said. "Now, Michelle, it's *you* we have to be concerned about. We're your family. You've spent quite enough time feeling sorry for Dora—most of elementary school I suppose it's been. Now that you're going into junior high school, you should learn to expand your... your horizons. It really is time for you two to, well, go your separate ways."

"Feeling *sorry* for Dora—me?" I fume. "Mama, Dora and I are friends! Who brought me my homework every day when I was sick for those two months in fourth grade? Faithful old Klutzy."

"What about all the mixed-up assignments?" interrupts Mama. "You ended up doing half that essay on the fur trade for her cousin, when you were supposed to be studying about ancient Babylon or some such thing."

15

"Klutzy was taking homework home to a couple of people just then—but I passed with good marks in the end, didn't I? That's what counts," I say with feeling.

"And remember all the letters Klutzy sent me while I was stuck there in bed? All the stories she wrote so I wouldn't be bored? And the crazy poetry to make me laugh?"

I search for another example of how indispensable Klutzy is. "Who taught the dog to fetch the newspaper for Dad?"

"Yes," agrees Mama, "And we haven't been able to decipher a headline for over two years."

"C'mon, Mama," I plead. "You really can't blame Klutzy. Woofy's just developed an appetite for the printed word because he's such a smart dog, that's all."

Mama sighs.

I push on: "Klutzy has been a great help around here—she always keeps an eye on the place when we're away on vacations. She never forgets to water the plants..."

Mama's face totally clouds and I'm sorry I used that last example. Our family has lost a lot of good plants on account of Klutzy's being so faithful. When it comes to using a watering can, Klutzy's motto seems to be: 'If some is good, more is better.'

"She takes care of the plants, all right," says Mama, darkly. "And her efforts are exactly a case in point. Dora *is* a dear—she means well—but everything she does turns out all wrong. My own mother was fond of reminding me that 'birds of a feather flock together.' You'll be considered the same type as Dora—a strange duck—if you continue to chum with her. Terez seems to think those ruffians in junior high school will tar and feather both you and Dora if you're together. And quite frankly, Michelle, I can see that Terez has a point."

"Mo—ther!" I moan.

"Don't interrupt me now, Michelle. I feel that I'm to blame for your relationship with Dora ever having started. Remember when you first brought Dora home to meet me? I nearly fainted when I saw her. I mean, she's not just homely, she's...well, she's almost freakish with those crossed eyes and that clumsy way she has of walking."

"So you want me to find a friend who can win a beauty contest."

"You're just being contrary," snaps Mama. "You know, I'm sure you chose Dora as a friend because we'd teased you so long about your looks. Your own family had...had destroyed your self-image. But by the time I realized what we'd done, it was too late—you were already such good friends with Dora."

I try to sound impressed: "Mama, do

you get your theories from Ann Landers, or do you make up this stuff all by yourself?"

Mama persists: "Really, Michelle! It's true. We hadn't wanted you to become conceited. But we teased you until your sense-of-self was completely off. Just look into a mirror. Surely you can see for yourself now. I hope you know that you deserve a *bright-looking, attractive* friend—not Dora."

"Oh, brother!" I groan.

"Besides," Mama continues, undaunted. "I'm not at all happy about you being associated with that family any more. Dora's father—well, people are beginning to talk. He drinks, and very heavily from what I've heard. And you know her older sister was charged with shoplifting..."

This dagger of Mama's makes me go a little wild: "But Klutzy's not like her Dad or that mixed-up sister of hers!" She only drinks martinis and limits her stealing to color TVs and microwaves."

"Michelle Leland, I will *not* have you be obstinate!" reprimands Mama. "Just you remember: 'A man is known by the company he keeps.' And that goes for a woman too—or girl, as the case may be."

Mama gets up to leave, looking as if she's won another open and shut case.

I burst out: "And who do you want Klutzy to keep company with? The class boa constrictor?"

Mama reddens. "Don't make this harder than it already is, Michelle. I'm fond of Dora. But for your own good, I must ask you, *now*, to make another best friend for school. You're finished with sixth grade and elementary school—finish with Dora Klutzmann too. Put away childish things..."

"Or to put it another way," I add coldly, "Drop Dora Klutzmann on her head."

"Put it any way you please," snaps Mama as she marches out of my room. "Just call it quits. As of now. And *that's* an *order!*"

I *sieg heil* to her back as she slams the door shut.

"*Ja wohl!*" I shout, trying to remember how they respond to commands in the Hitler movies.

But I get the sinking feeling that the last laugh is really on Klutzy and me.

Chapter Three

MAKING COMPARISONS

"**M**AY I have your attention, please!" Mr. Numble yells for the third time into the microphone.

Pretty well all us new seventh grade kids canned it the first minute the principal opened his mouth. But out of the corner of my eye I can see a crowd of ninth graders sitting high in the bleachers. They're still popping bubbles and laughing hysterically. As if the first day back at school is some tremendous joke.

"It must be excellent to be in ninth grade," my new friend Bonnie hisses in my ear.

"They don't impress me," I say coolly.

Bonnie looks slammed. Like I put ice cubes down her back. She looks straight ahead, up at Mr. Numble. He's finally giving the ninth graders a blast.

"It is the responsibility of our senior

class to set an example..." Blah, blah, blah.

I know now why Terez calls him 'Bumble Numble.' As I watch ol' Bumble I can see the impersonations Terez used to do of him at home. The neck jerk is right on. The erratic twitch of his chin. The furrowed brow and hunted look as his eyes dart around in their sockets.

I muffle a laugh into my fist and Bonnie gives me a puzzled half-smile. She blushes a little, like maybe I'm laughing at *her*.

I get control of my face and whisper, "I'll tell you later."

Beginning a friendship is hard. Bonnie is pretty, with caramel-colored hair and shiny blue eyes. She's busy with the Young People's Group, so we don't get a whole lot of time together. But our lockers are side by side, and we have most of our classes together. I've found that Bonnie can be loads of fun. She's always ready for a laugh.

Trouble is, we're nowhere near understanding each other yet. We're not 'in rhythm;' not reading each other's minds. We never say anything at *exactly* the same time.

Not like Dora Klutzmann and me. It seemed Klutzy and I were always cracking up about things. And we never had to explain the joke to each other—we just *knew*.

I sigh. I think about the good times with Klutzy. Ordering cola and chips at the mall every Saturday afternoon. Searching for a big cigar butt in an ash tray, and leaving it hanging from the yellow-green teeth of the two-headed calf in the Farm Museum. Buying rabbit feed cheap at the Co-op and loading our air guns to fire pellets down on trains passing under the Ninth Street bridge. I guess things will get like that with Bonnie—eventually.

But for now, here's Bonnie sitting beside me taking in every word that the principal lets drop. Like he's some top singer who's just dropped in from a tour. I mean, she's taking him seriously, for heaven's sake! Now if it were Klutzy and I together here, we would have been in hysterics by this time. Rolling in the aisle. Especially Klutz—she tends to trip and stumble even when she's not laughing.

Numble Bumble's stage show would

keep anyone in stitches. Just like Terez told me. And Bumble really *does* look like he's come in clown costume. He has an orange plaid sports jacket that can't hope to button up over his endless waistline, no matter how hard each of the stripes stretches. His shiny gold pants look as if they've been cut out of vinyl. Maybe to match the vinyl pen holder that juts out of his jacket pocket. I make a guess that the assorted pens have names on them like: *Joe Blow's Auto Body: We meet by accident*, or *Frank's Pizza Palace: We've got the bottoms; you choose the toppings*.

I think sadly to myself that Klutzy and I would have sat for hours making up corny names and slogans for pens like that.

Numble has said enough by this time. He gives his final, well-rehearsed lines: "Any problem you have, no matter how great or how small, is *my* problem too. A problem isn't a problem when it's solved, and together we can solve anything. This is a year for teamwork. So, *team*, let's get down to action!" Numble Bumble turns to sit down, a pleased glow on his bald crown.

A teacher hisses something to him. Bumble turns back to the mike. He over-steps it so that his enormous stomach hits the mike rod. The air crackles about our ears and roars as the mike crashes to the gym floor.

Bumble manages to get the mike back on its stand. He straightens himself as best his roundness allows and then rocks back and forth from his heels to his toes, shouting, "Order! Order now!"

Finally the clapping, whistling, and stomping is getting boring. It really wasn't all that funny.

Bumble coughs once as if that will do the trick: "Hrumph, ah, Ms. Dewmil has, er, kindly reminded me that everyone should have bus passes and cafeteria cards renewed."

As the herd rumbles out of the gym and back to home room, I can't help thinking about Bumble and Klutzy. And what Terez says about both of them being losers. I have to admit that even I—Klutzy's ex-best friend—can't help making comparisons.

Chapter Four

TO BE OR NOT TO BE

THE bottle of mouthwash sits brightly green on Ms. Dewmil's desk. I slump into my seat and hope she won't think any of us in the front row put it there.

It's a mean trick, I think. I wish Bonnie hadn't told me Frank was going to do this. How can I look innocent?

I look hard at my pencil. *Special Lead*, I read for the hundredth time. I vow that I'm not going to chew on my next pencil. It looks so grungy. I wonder if I can write with my fingers holding the very top where I've mangled the end near the eraser, instead of holding it down near the lead.

Pencils are crazy for junior high, I think to myself. But Dewmil insists on pencils for English composition.

Then, speak of the devil, in walks Ms.

Dewmil. Or *Mildew* as she is more commonly known.

She plunks her piles of papers down on the desk. The bottle of mouthwash flashes its cruel green eyes.

Mildew turns to us, and in her ancient, croaking whisper hisses, "Can anyone tell me *who...*"

I tense and bite into my pencil.

"...wrote 'To be or not to be; that is the question'?"

The whole class is so relieved that we all burst into uproarious laughter.

Mildew blinks and purses her thin lips.

She writes out the quote on the board and goes on doggedly about Shakespeare and poetry. I have to admire her fanatic interest in writing. I also have to give her credit for the way she ignores the mouthwash bottle winking away in the sunshine.

Personally, I think Frank is a rat for all the mean things he thinks up. I really wonder how Bonnie can be so crazy about him. Pickings at the Young People's Group must be pretty slim. Maybe she thinks Frank's wonderful because her parents think he's terrible. Who knows? I sure can't figure it out.

I squirm inside when I recall all the things I've gotten into with Bonnie and Frank. They do things for laughs—nothing too far out, just some things that are kind of mean. Pranks really, I console myself. Jokes, that's all. I have to get involved, too, or else Bonnie will think I'm a goody-goody and get fed up with me.

Just like Terez said, when it comes right down to it, you've got to belong to some group at this school. Or else. And since, as it is, I'm already on the 'lunatic fringe,' I'd better play along with Bonnie and Frank...

"Michelle! I asked you to pass those papers back," breathes Mildew heavily in my face. I wilt from the fumes. I wonder if she'll eventually decide to use the mouthwash.

I scramble to pass the stack of papers back. Then I hurriedly write my name in the top right-hand corner.

When Mildew tours round to the back of the class, I whisper frantically to Bonnie: "What are we supposed to be doing? I was thinking about something else—didn't hear what Mildew said."

"Poetry—a poem about a time in your

life when you *did* or did *not* answer *the question*," and Bonnie rolls her eyes.

"Huh?" I puzzle.

But Mildew is on to us: "You two work *now* or in detention time. Which is it going to be?" she snaps.

Now she leans over my shoulder to see what I've written. She harumphs and moves on.

My eyes rivet on the lined paper. It's foolscap, the extra long kind that takes forever to fill.

"Hmm," my brain creaks. "When did I ever face the question 'To be or not to be?'"

My mind is haunted by Klutzy. Pictures of our past friendship pass like ghosts before my eyes.

"To be or not to be...a friend," I think painfully. I begin to write—suddenly—from my heart.

Chapter Five

BEFORE THE COCK CROWS, THOU SHALT DENY ME

"**W**HO do you think you are?" jeers Frank at me. "Lady Muck? Hey, group, this here is Lady Muck from now on."

Frank's two lame-brained friends snicker, and Carolanne hee haws. I wish I could crawl into my locker and never be with this bunch of louts again. Most of all, I wish I could control the heat waves of red I feel wafting up my face.

"Oh, Frank," whines Bonnie. "C'mon. Let's just *forget* it."

Frank turns on her, too. "What d'ya mean, forget it! This moaner has been down on every idea I come up with."

My red blush is finally turning into anger. "Strain your brain and think,

Frank. I haven't ever said anything about all the other..."

"Said?" roars Frank. "No, you don't 'said' nothing. It's the 'holier-than-thou' looks and..."

"Pardon me for breathing!" I snap.

Frank is getting really angry now. "Always the big-shot talker, but you're just a dirty little..."

"Frank, calm down! The teachers are going to hear us," hisses Bonnie. I feel kind of proud of her for at least stepping in between Frank and me. "You don't even know why Mitch is down on this idea to corner Klutzmann. Maybe she's got good reasons of her own. Weren't you best friends with Dora Klutzmann once, Mitch?"

Frank's jaw drops. Every eye is instantly on me.

"*You* were a friend of creepy Dora Klutzmann's?" goos Carolanne. Like I'm maybe related to Godzilla.

I feel another hot blush flood my cheeks. "Friends? Nope. We were never friends."

Bonnie looks embarrassed and confused. "Oh, uh, I thought you used to walk home with her..."

"Bonnie!" I try to give her a look that says 'Can it, will you?' "Dora Klutzmann lives near me, that's all. We used to walk together once in a while. So what?"

"Figures," leers Frank. "That's where you learned to walk knock-kneed, eh, Mitch?"

Frank, the bozo comedian. Getting laughs by putting everybody else down. But his humor doesn't amuse me. It only makes me think how pleasant it would be to kick him.

"All I want to know is *why* you have to go after Dora Klutzmann?" I demand, exasperated. "I can see maybe getting at Mildew the way you do. And I guess Bumble deserves it. But why poor ol' Klutzy?"

"Klutzy, eh?" sneers Carolanne. "That's a perfect description for her."

"*Her*, nothing. Klutzmann is an *it*," Frank interrupts. "Lady Muck wants to know why *it* has been chosen to receive my personal attention."

"I know," says Brad, Frank's right-hand man. "It's Klutzmann's personality—she can charm slugs right out of the grass."

"And her face," laughs Bonnie. "It's

enough to make a baby cry."

"Eat your heart out, Frankenstein," Carolanne whoops.

Frank puts in his two-bits' worth: "Her vital statistics drive me wild."

I cut off his brilliant wit: "You're not

exactly 'playmate-of-the-month' yourself, Frank."

He takes a menacing step towards me. "Come to think of it, Lady Muck, your face could stand a good rearranging."

Suddenly Mr. Samoraki, the biology teacher, descends on our group like a kamikaze pilot. "OK, kids. Move it! The bell's about to ring."

"Whew, saved!" I think as I scoop my books up off the floor.

"Not so fast, Lady Muck," growls Frank. "The action-plan for Klutzmann is still on." He sweeps a commanding gaze at the other kids: "Right, group?"

"Sure, Frank."

"Yeah."

"OK."

"Right."

Frank looks smug. He turns to me with a threatening glint in his eye. "So now how are your plans to get chummy with Klutzmann again?"

"I never was chummy with her," I shout, "and I never will be. Satisfied?"

"We'll see how you do tomorrow, Lady Muck. You just better take care of your share of the action. We'll see *then*."

I run for my class, but really I'm running from Frank. The bully. The jerk.

"But who's the jerk, really?" a voice in my head rants. *"Three times* you told them you were never Klutzy's friend."

Chapter Six

SINCERELY, KLUTZY

THE letter drops from my locker gratings with a soft flop onto the floor.

Bonnie is off at the water fountain with loud-mouth Frank. I'm secretly hoping Frank will drown there sometime before this afternoon's caper.

I know right away that the letter is from Klutzy. I could tell her scrawl anywhere.

I read, with a thudding, sick feeling in my throat:

Dear Mitch,

    I guess I can understand your folks telling you who you can and can't chum with. My Dad once said I couldn't play with a little kid down the street who kept using bad words. It just hurts me that I'm the one to be excluded from your friendship. (I keep wondering if your Mom thinks all her plants died because I was saying dirty words to them or something. Honest, Mitch, it was just too much water, that's all!)

I'm finding junior high tough. How about you? In fact, life is the pits. But, well, there's nothing you can do so I'll quit moaning. It's the story of my life anyway— except for you. You were the best thing that ever happened to me, Mitch.

Would it be OK if I write to you? It would be almost like talking. Whenever I've phoned, Terez says you're not home. I can take a hint. Phone calls are out too, right? But a letter wouldn't hurt, would it? You don't have to write back if you don't want to but, just in case, my locker number is 182B.

You would have been proud of the detective work I've done to find your locker. Like the good old days.

Remember our old 'Arther's Club?' (I always laugh at our spelling.) How about we start it up again? I've got some poetry I've been writing, and it would be great if you'd take a look at it.

The poem stapled to this letter is one I just finished. I thought of it during a TV commercial while I was contemplating a late-night peanut butter sandwich.

You know how everything on TV is 'new, improved' this or that? Always changing. Just like people—always changing; so-called 'improving.' (Though from what I've seen, getting older doesn't always mean getting better.)

But peanut butter—well, it never changes. You can count on it to be the same old comforting friend you always knew. So I called the poem "Peanut Butter Is Forever." What d'you think?

Well, I guess I'd better sign off. I hope you don't mind me writing to you. I sure miss you, Mitch.

I mean this.

Sincerely,
Klutzy

Chapter Seven

DUE DAY

"**M**ITCH," repeats Bonnie. "Aren't you going to answer?"

"Huh? Answer?" I say, surprised. Has Bonnie been half reading my thoughts? I've been thinking about how to answer Klutzy's letter.

"Yes, answer me. Wow, you're really out to lunch today!" sniffs Bonnie.

"Not out to lunch," I smile. "I'm just thinking about the lasting qualities of peanut butter."

Bonnie looks at me as if I've gone totally whacko. "C'mon, let's hurry and get to English," she sighs. We speed up our pace.

I try starting a normal conversation: "Uh, Bonnie, what were you asking me when I didn't answer you?"

"I've been trying to find out what you wrote for the take-home exam. You know, the writing for Mildew. It's due today."

I stop dead in my tracks. "Today?" I shriek. "That take-home is due on Thursday!"

"Nope," says Bonnie confidently. She distinctly reminds me of the store clerks who seem so smugly pleased when they don't happen to have something that you desperately need. "The take-home writing exam is due today, Wednesday. It's the biology project that's due Thursday. Don't tell me you haven't got your writing done, you dope," she goes on ruthlessly. "Mildew is going to destroy you."

Sometimes I feel that Bonnie and Frank deserve each other. This is definitely one of those moments.

"Thanks for the info, pal," I say grimly. "Why didn't you tell me about this yesterday?"

"I'm not your baby-sitter, sweetie," Bonnie squeaks. She makes a funny face.

I have two urges—either to slug her or to laugh. So I laugh. She laughs with me.

The bell clamors and we sprint to make it to class on time.

"Why am I in such a hurry?" I think as I sink, breathless, into my desk. "Here's me running to meet certain death—like a lame-brained lemming."

I have time to stew because Mildew hasn't arrived yet. She always makes a late entrance into English class. We've all taken a guess as to where she must be between bell and official entrance time.

My guess is that she's in the ladies' room rolling her ankle socks just so. Mildew has got to be the only person in the world who wears ankle socks over support hose.

Bonnie says that Mildew is probably a closet smoker taking a last drag before class.

But it's Terez, of course, who has the facts. According to her, Mildew used to come early to all her classes. Then one group of kids locked her in her classroom and took off. It happened just before last period, and Mildew wasn't rescued until late that night when the custodian came round to clean.

Terez knows all the gossip and rumors and facts.

Me—I don't even know what most of the assignments are. And due dates are my downfall. Like today—good grief!

I listlessly flop open my binder. There before my eyes is Klutzy's envelope staring up at me like a little miracle. "The poem!" I gasp to myself. "Klutzy's poetry is fantastic."

My mind flashes back to an old Humphrey Bogart movie. The heroine was freed at the last minute, and she laughed and cried and slobbered all over Bogey's jacket.

I thought that scene was pure cornball—but that's exactly what I feel like now: laughing and crying all at once. In a mad frenzy I copy out Klutzy's poem.

"Peanut Butter Is Forever" by Michelle Leland. Student number 473-912.

Chapter Eight

OUT TO GET KLUTZY

S O THIS is the basement pit and good ol' 182B. The locker where I should be delivering a thank you note to Klutzy for saving my life in English class. Instead, here I am with this weird bunch who are out to jam her *into* her locker. I need my head read. I rub my fingertips over my forehead to ease the headache of mixed-up feelings twisting around in my brain.

"You OK, Mitch?" whispers Bonnie. "C'mon, this is just for a laugh, you know."

"You wouldn't be laughing if it was *you* being stuffed into the locker," I growl back.

"Shut up, you two," hisses Frank. "We don't know which stairs Klutzmann'll come down, and she should be here any minute."

The basement hall is dim and dingy. The perfect setting for a Hitchcock movie. The smell of dirty socks and rotten bananas hangs in the air like bad breath.

182B—the B must stand for basement, bad luck, and better luck next time, Klutzy, I think mournfully. Better luck with your family, friends, looks, and locker space. I look around at the depressing hall. I'd hate to start and end my day down here in this dungeon.

I vaguely wonder about the theory of coming back for a second life in another body. Klutzy sure deserves something better than what she has now. She really seems to have nothing going for her, and she's a nobody.

But what about me, good ol' pal Michelle—am I a somebody? Oh sure, I'm really making it in junior high. Right in the middle of Frank Flatsam's 'in-crowd.' Big deal!

The only thing I'm truly 'in' on is the plan to get Klutzy. I rehearse Frank's nasty plan in my brain:

• First, Carolanne accuses Klutzy of stealing pencils in Mildew's class. Klutzy gets a detention, so she comes to her locker when everyone else has cleared out and gone home. . . . done.

- Second, Frank gets Klutzy's attention when she comes down the stairs; so that,

- Third, Bonnie and Larry sneak up the opposite stairs and circle around behind Klutzy. They wait at the exit where she'll try to escape Frank.

- Fourth, Bonnie and Larry grab her and drag her over to the rest of us; and,

- Fifth, we all jam her into her locker, slam the door shut, and lock her in.

My own *personal* part of the plan is:

- Sixth, secretly let Klutzy out after the others leave.

"That way, I'll at least be a little help," I console myself. I know Klutzy won't die or anything—even if she stayed there all night. She could still breathe—with all those little vent holes in the front. But . . . poor old Klutz!

"Here she comes now," giggles Carol-anne nervously.

I peer out from my hiding place and look towards the far end of the hall. Klutzy is taking her last step down the stairs. She stumbles, drops a book, and slowly picks it up.

"If there *is* a second chance at life," I

muse, "I doubt if Klutzy'll come back as a ballerina."

It seems as if time stands still. I look at Klutzy, and see what she really looks like. Her hangdog look; her tacky green sweater; her frumpy, too long skirt. I see she's let her skinny brown hair get long and greasy.

"She looks beaten and lumpy, like a mini-Mildew," I think sadly. "Who knows, maybe Mildew started like Klutzy. Great in English class, but a junior high reject. Alone and unloved. Hounded by bullies like Frank..."

Frank glides out of hiding and leans, all smooth and oily, against the lockers at our end of the hall. Bonnie and Larry disappear like ghosts up the stairs behind me.

Frank calls down to Klutzy: "Hey, scab face, what ragbag did you get your fancy threads from? Couldn't have been Dan's Used Duds shop. Didn't they tell ya that you shouldn't go digging in the garbage cans out back?"

Klutzy cuts in, her voice shaky and high. "Look, you; I don't know who you are or what your problem is, but you've been on my case since the first day of junior high. You'd better leave me alone or..."

"Or what, dog biscuit? You gonna tell your old man to phone the school? I hear he's never sober enough to dial..."

I've heard enough. This is too much! My blood is thudding, choking my throat. Who does this Frank creep think he is?! This is my *friend* he's insulting. My friend, Klutzy.

My legs catapult me out from the doorway where I'm hiding. I'm in the middle of the corridor screaming, "Klutzy, run up to the office. Not the exit door. Frank is gonna..."

I feel a rough hand clamp over my mouth. I bite for all I'm worth. Then I feel a thud and a burst of pain. Everybody is yelling 'cause Frank is slugging me.

But the important thing for me, in that second before I see stars, is the brief glimpse I've caught of Klutzy clattering up the stairs at the far end of the dark hallway.

Chapter Nine

I'M FAMOUS – NOW WHAT'LL I DO?

I wince through my black eye as I stare at the bulletin board. My eye is not the only thing that's hurting me.

"How can Mildew do this to me?" I moan. "Display that poem with *my* name on it! 'Peanut Butter Is Forever' by Michelle Leland—if Klutzy sees this before I explain it to her, she'll hate me forever."

Someone comes up behind me and stands staring at the board.

"My life is over," I think glumly. "Klutzy's gonna despise me. Bonnie won't talk to me. Frank is probably still furious, even though he did land me with a shiner. And besides all this, Mildew is out to make me famous. That's the sign of a real loser."

The person beside me turns to go, but then wheels around towards me. "Hey!"

he says enthusiastically. "Are *you* Terez Leland's sister?"

"Not in public, I'm not," I say. I slowly turn my swollen face, only to see this gorgeous hunk at my side!

He's tall; nice and solid, but not too beefy; dark-brown hair kind of wild and curly; gray-blue eyes like smoke from a fire; a twisty, warm grin showing toothpaste ad teeth. Not to mention the designer jeans.

My knees buckle and my blood pressure skyrockets. "Uh, oh," I stammer, "er, only at home I *have* to be—her sister, that is. But how did you know that Terez is my sister?"

The Hunk beams down at me. "I was at the senior high interviewing the cheerleaders this morning. One, named Terez Leland, told me to be on the look-out for her kid sister here at Clearview. She told me that 'junior' walked into a door last night. And you're the only one around here who fits the description she gave."

My heart sinks. My killing instinct rises. Just wait until I get some goods on Terez that I can blab around. My only consolation is that I've bamboozled her into believing my phony story about this black eye. For the first time in her life, Terez doesn't have the full scoop.

I grimace. "I'll bet she gave some account—Terez is great at elaborating details. Well, see you around."

"Wait a minute," and the Hunk touches my arm.

"A minute?" I think. "For you, I'd wait the rest of my life." I mean, this guy is a knockout, and here he is talking to *me*, a nobody seventh grader!

"Since you're Terez Leland's sister, does that mean your name is Michelle?" he asks.

I blush through my purple bruises, right up to the black eye. But, as usual, I can't control my mouth. "And who are you? Sherlock Holmes?"

He grins. "Oh, me? I'm Tim Winscott."

"You mean the Tim Winscott who is a football star and editor of the Alexander Henry/Clearview *Herald*?" I gasp.

"That's me," Tim smirks. "I just do detective work on the side."

"And you wear a big S on your T-shirt and change in a telephone booth, right?"

"You guessed it—but those clear glass booths are driving me crazy."

We laugh. At least he laughs, and I melt

into a pool at his feet. I try to pull my thoughts together. "How do you know that my name is Michelle?" I ask.

"From here, on the bulletin board. The author of this poem, 'Peanut Butter Is Forever,' has the same last name as Terez. Your writing is terrific. I'm impressed."

"Oh, thanks," I stammer. "But I'm not *that* good."

"Now don't get modest on me," says Tim. "This is darn good writing. You see, I need a poetry columnist for the *Herald*. How about it?"

"Oh *no*, really. What I mean is..."

The bell rings for class and Tim turns to leave.

"I may even throw in a junior editor position," he calls over his shoulder. "I can see that you drive a hard bargain. Meet me at the *Herald* office tomorrow after school. We'll talk."

"Oh, gorgeous Tim," I mourn silently. "We may talk, but you're just going to end up being another on my growing list of ex-fans."

Chapter Ten

TEREZ ON THE SCENE

TEREZ is just ahead of me in the noon hour crowd drifting towards the parking lot. She's swaying along and jingling the car keys, chatting with her friend, Di, as if they had all the time in the world.

"How do you two ever get home for lunch and back to school in time?" I ask as I join them.

Di doesn't even turn her head, and Terez briefly looks through me. "Wheels, kid," she says.

I feel like a fly who's been told to buzz off.

I have to admire Terez's double concentration. She can keep up her end of the conversation—a continuous stream of monosyllabic grunts—while at the same time maintaining a steady surveillance of the parking lot to check out the action.

"Terez has got it together," I think hopefully. "Maybe she'll help me out of this mess."

I fondly remember the one time in my life when Terez protected me. I was a real little kid, and the crowd at the skating rink door was nearly trampling me. Terez fought like a wildcat and got me up in her arms like a mother with her baby.

"Hey, Terez, remember the time at the skating rink?" I blurt out, trying to make an opening for myself in the conversation.

Di slowly turns her well-groomed brunette head my way. She makes me feel that maybe I've turned green and have antennae sticking out of my ears.

Terez looks bugged. "What *are* you blabbering about, Mitch?" she says, exasperated. "Go to the cafeteria and play with your little friends."

"But I want to go home for lunch today, Terez. Could I get a ride with you? Please!" I say desperately.

Terez oozes with disdain: "You think I want to be seen with you in *my* car?" She doesn't add *creep* but she might as well.

I want to scream that it's Mama's car, not Terez's. But I try to keep a pleading, hopeful face.

Di adjusts her sun glasses. "I'll leave you to the infant division, Terez. Talk to you later," and she swaggers off.

Maybe Terez will pay more attention to me now. She always puts on the big shot act when Di is around.

"How can you stand that dopey Dianna?" I ask Terez as we walk over to the car. "All she's got going for her is that over-sized bust of hers. Poor, deformed creature."

"You rude brat!" says Terez. "She just happens to be *the* top cheerleader." But I notice the beginning of a smirk lurking behind Terez's bronzed coral lips. "Get in then, Mitch. And put on the paper bag."

I moan: "Aw, c'mon, Terez. Not that again."

Terez is adamant. "If you want a ride with me, in the middle of the day, in broad daylight, you wear the bag!"

I know from experience there's no use arguing this one. I get into the car and meekly pull the big brown paper bag out of the glove compartment. I slump down in the seat as Terez turns the key in the ignition. If anyone asks her later, "Who was the brown bag with you at lunch?", she'll have no hesitation in naming me. That's all I'd need to further my fame.

"Terez, I've got a problem," I say as we drive off.

"Speak up, Mitch. I can't hear you," says Terez.

I have to shout through the brown bag. "I have a problem!"

"You're telling me!" Terez deadpans. "You've had a problem since you were two years old."

"Very funny," I mumble. "Look, Terez, I didn't walk into a door yesterday like I told Mama. I got slugged by Frank Flatsam."

"What?" gasps Terez. "That little two-bit gangster. I've half a mind to..."

At least now I've got my sister's full attention.

"But my real problem is that Tim Winscott wants me to work on the *Herald*."

"*That* is not a problem," gooes Terez, suddenly transfixed by the name of a gorgeous male. "Tim Winscott is a darling. You'll make the big time, kid, working with him on the *Herald*."

"But it's a problem if the writing he thinks is mine isn't mine," I say sadly.

"Well, whose writing is it?" Terez demands.

"I'd rather not say," and I'm glad the paper bag is hiding my red face.

"Then I'd rather not help you," says Terez, all snippy.

"Terez," I plead. "I can't tell you. It might prejudice any brilliant ideas you'd have to help me. All I can say is that the writer is a kid at school who helped me stay out of trouble with Mildew."

Terez is not overfond of Mildew. She is silent as the signal light clicks the moments away. Then she burns rubber on the turn.

"Mama told you that ruins the tires," I blurt out.

"Shut up. I'm thinking," commands Terez. "Honestly, you make such a big deal out of things, Mitch. You should have told the truth in the first place, and you'd be OK now."

"Oh, you're brilliant, Terez," I say dryly. "Can you offer me any more pearls of wisdom?"

"It's a fact," persists Terez. "What's the old saying? 'Truth conquers all.'"

"I believe Mama says 'LOVE conquers all,'" I correct.

"They're both good sayings," Terez concludes lightly. The car engine dies. "We're home. Take off the bag before Mom sees it."

"What's the matter?" I gibe. "Doesn't truthful old Terez want her Mommy to see the truth."

"Quiet, or you'll walk back to school," she snaps.

I was counting on Terez's advice, and all she can do is reel off clichés.

"Thanks for all your help, sweet sister," I say bitterly. "Maybe I should tell Tim about your talents. You could write a brilliant Dear Doris column for the *Herald*."

"Sure, anytime," she says breezily.

"Oh, Terez, please don't say anything about this to Mama, OK? It's a private problem."

Terez sweeps open the back porch door. "Listen, kid, every problem in life is a private problem."

Spoken like a true Abigail Van Buren. Dear Abby, Dear Doris: eat your hearts out....Terez is on the scene.

Chapter Eleven

TAKING COUNSEL

"G O HOME for lunch?" asks Bonnie as she clangs her locker door shut. I'm still rummaging around for my math text.

"Yeah—got a ride with my sister," I mutter.

"Maybe you should get a ride home all the time," Bonnie says mysteriously.

I look at her quizzically, but she looks away. "What's the matter? Did they burn the spaghetti again?" I ask. "That cafeteria is the pits."

"It's deadly, all right—but it's gonna be more than deadly for you if you're not careful!" Bonnie's voice is low and husky. Her china blue eyes dart around the hall, as if on the lookout. Then she starts walking away.

"Hey, wait a minute!" I grab her arm. "What's all this James Bond talk about 'deadly'? Is someone planning to poison me or something?"

Bonnie peers nervously up and down the hall. "I'm not supposed to say anything—but, oh, Mitch!" Now Bonnie looks completely miserable. "Frank says you're really in for it. He says you're due for a second black eye..."

"Ha!" I laugh feebly. "Maybe then I'll be able to write an essay for Mildew on 'The Life and Times of a Migratory Raccoon.'"

Bonnie isn't amused. "This is serious, Mitch. Frank is still furious with you over that Dora Klutzmann mess-up. I told him he and I are quits if he goes after you any more, but Frank says...oh-oh—look out, Michelle. Hide in the girls' can! That's one of Frank's guys coming. I'll say you've already gone to math."

Bonnie walks away fast and I dive for the john next to our lockers. I latch the cubicle door and sit on the toilet lid with my knees drawn up to my chin. (I saw it done once in a detective movie. That way, your feet don't give you away.) I don't move a muscle until the one o'clock bell rings. The hall quiets down.

My brain boggles—where should I hide? Not here forever. Frank's group includes girls who'll search the johns.

And I can't go home either. Knowing Frank, he probably has somebody watching the exits.

I quickly bob my head out the washroom door to check the hall. Empty. But where do I go from here?

The counseling area on the top floor is usually deserted. And behind the pillar used for notices and junk, there's a big old-fashioned alcove for the fire extinguisher. I beat a hasty retreat up the stairs.

I wedge myself in as far as I can behind the fire extinguisher. I push and squeeze until I find I can't move any more at all— not farther in, and not out either.

The time ticks away. One minute, a minute and a half; fifty years later it's maybe a minute and three-quarters.

I decide, resolutely, that I need help. At this point, I'm willing to listen to free advice from anyone.

It occurs to me that there's always prayer. I'm getting a little old for "Now I lay me down to sleep"—there's got to be another one. Of course, I know some graces that we say for dinner, but I just can't bring myself to say one.

Then, who should walk by but a miniature angel of mercy! Mrs. Small, one of our school counselors. All the kids call her the Shrink. Not only is she just a shrimp in her tallest heels, but she made the fatal mistake of telling Terez's class that fifteen years of her teaching had been in first grade—Mrs. Shrink and the little shrinks! Even with a bad start like that though, there's something about the Shrink you can't help liking.

Of course, only the real far-outs ever get caught in her counseling office, but lots of kids stop her in the hall for a five minute chat. She's got a nice motherly way about her. She ooohs and aaahhs in the right places; moans when it's appropriate—you know what I mean. Her big brown eyes are pools of "I'm listening; let me help you." I don't know if you learn that in Shrink School; I mean, do eye exercises or something, but whatever it takes, the Shrink has it.

"Psst, Mrs. Small, do you think I could talk to you for a minute?" I hiss.

Shrink lurches to a halt and peers around to find out where the voice has come from. "Why, Michelle, that's you back there, isn't it? *How* did you manage to squeeze in behind that fire extinguisher?"

"Wasn't easy," I groan.

"Do you think you'll be able to get out of there, dear? Can I help?" Shrink warms me with those brown eyes full of concern.

"Oh, I'll get out somehow—no problem," I hiccup. Then when Shrink looks doubtful and even more worried, I add: "Course, I might just as well stay here for life."

"Goodness!" gasps Shrink. "Michelle, if this is some new way to enforce a starvation diet..."

"No, ma'am, this is no fad. And I wasn't on a diet the day you were on duty in the lunch room..."

"Yes, I know," recalls Shrink. "You threw away your sandwiches because they were corned beef, and you only like the lasting quality of peanut butter."

"Hey, those were my exact words!" I laugh.

"Uh-huh," smiles Shrink. "Now I want your exact words on why you're up here stuck behind that extinguisher."

"Well, Mrs. Small, this is my only escape. I don't dare leave here, *or* go home, because I'll end up with two black eyes instead of this one," I begin.

Shrink squares her little shoulders and draws herself up to her full height. She looks ready for battle, putting her hand protectively on my one protruding shoulder.

"Michelle, are you telling me that your parents beat you?"

"Oh, no, ma'am!" I sputter.

"Then who?" counters Shrink.

"I don't want to mention names," I say miserably. "I just want some advice."

"A beating is a beating, and I want to know who is threatening you," says Shrink firmly. "Are you sure you're not covering for your parents?"

Looks as if I only have two choices: to encourage a lawsuit on my family, or to fink on Frank.

I look pleadingly at Shrink. "It's *not* my parents—honest. It's someone here at school. He wants to smash me a second time because I ruined his plan to get Dora Klutzmann."

"Hmm," growls Shrink. "I could name at least two possible gorillas on that score. But if you're decided on no names, that's up to you, I suppose."

She thinks hard a minute, and then

gets all business-like. "First, we have to get you out of this hiding place..."

"Gee, thanks, Mrs. Small. It *is* kind of tight in here." I don't mention that I can hardly breathe and all my ribs feel bruised.

"Then how about coming next door to my office and telling me the whole story?" grunts Shrink as she tugs on my arm to get me out.

"Not your *office!*" I shriek, partly from the pain of her pulls, and partly 'cause I'm terrified of getting an even more loony reputation.

I come away from the alcove with a sudden jolt—sending myself, the Shrink, and the fire extinguisher flying. That harmless looking, little red tank goes beserk—foam squizzles everywhere. Shrink leaps on it, but obviously isn't familiar with the latest fire-fighting techniques. All she manages to do is point the wild nozzle in my face. When it registers that I'm beginning to look like a banana-cream pie, Shrink whoops with laughter and haphazardly aims the nozzle at the bulletin board and then the ceiling. The tiles rain white foam.

By the time the extinguisher loses its

zing, Shrink and I look like the Abominable Snowman's drippy cousins, just wandering in from an unfortunate expedition to the South Pole.

Shrink dismounts the now dead red zinger. She brushes the foam off her sagging dress and tries to sound back in control of things: "Now, Michelle, you need help."

I look mournfully at her through the cream-puff foam on my face and say, defeated, "Yes, ma'am."

Suddenly Shrink howls with laughter. "Correction," she gasps. "*We* need help."

Shrink makes an effort to pull herself together. "I'll get the custodian to come mop or vacuum, or whatever one does to a mess like this. And Mr. Numble needs to be told. As for you, Michelle, where are you supposed to be this afternoon? I can send around some notes to excuse you from classes."

"Er, math and study hall," I stammer, not quite believing my good fortune.

"I have all free periods this afternoon, so we're set," smiles Shrink. "I'll just take care of those classes of yours. You go change into dry clothes. Get your gym stuff on and meet me in the science project room—you know, at the back of the lab?"

"Sure, I know where..." But my voice sounds a little sick, as visions of Frank's fists and black eyes rise before me.

Without another word, a look of understanding passes over Shrink's foam-spattered face.

"On second thought, let's walk together to your locker," she says softly. "And the project room is not far from my office anyway. You can change in the lab and wait for me while I write the excuse notes. How about making coffee for us?"

"Make coffee—in the science room?" I echo. I vaguely feel as if I'm dreaming.

"Yes. Ms. Prundle and I have a little Bunsen burner and beaker set up in there. We can do everything except cappucino, and we're working on that. She's the brilliant one, really. I add the homey touches—you know, Scandinavian glass cups, linen napkins, and silver service. Real cream and not that foul powdered stuff...."

Shrink prattles on like this until we get to my locker. I fish around for my gym clothes. She keeps chattering all the way to the science room.

"Nobody likes to come to my counseling office—this lab is where I bring everyone for a chat," Shrink goes on. "Can't say I blame anyone. Hard as I've tried to civilize that office, it's no more than a broom closet, really. And then there's Mrs. Cinders from history—she can hear everything over the partition if she happens to be in her cubicle. Not very private for chatting about personal matters...."

Shrink disappears and I set up the Bunsen burner the way she's just shown me. Takes a while to grind the coffee beans with a mortar and pestle, but Shrink says she likes her coffee fresh from the bean. The aroma of 'Kenya's Best' soon conquers the pungent disinfectant odor floating around the lab.

It makes me recall drinking coffee at Klutzy's house whenever her Mom and Dad weren't home. Come to think of it, they were seldom home. Ah, the good old days!

Shrink appears again, this time in a pink flannel jogging suit and pink Adidas. Now she looks *really* short. And the track suit emphasizes her cuddly, motherly roundness. She's just the type to have little kids perched on her knee.

"Did all those little first graders you used to teach like sitting on your lap?" I blurt out.

"As a matter of fact, they did!" Shrink chuckles. "Ah, I'll never live down my first grade reputation! The word passes around here from generation to generation."

She climbs up on a lab stool beside me. "Enough about me. You know who I talked to in the office just now...?" She dumps a generous slurp of cream into her coffee.

Klutzy and I used to answer questions like this with: "Who? Mickey Mouse?" Or we'd say, "Is this a knock-knock joke?" I choke and get coffee up my nose thinking about it.

Shrink smiles. "Glad to see you're getting your sense of humor back—private as it may be. Anyway, I saw Mr. Numble."

"Nice to hear he's still in action." I venture a grin.

Shrink nods. "I know what you mean. But Michelle, you know, appearances aren't everything—Mr. Numble's quite an amazing man, really. I misjudged him at first, too. But I've found over the years that it's the *inside* and not the *outside* that counts with a person like him."

I look deep into my muddy coffee. "I'm beginning to learn *that*—you know, that appearances aren't everything."

Shrink waits. Then, "Want to talk about that?"

"No," I mumble. "Don't think so." And I gulp some more brew.

Shrink carries on, unperturbed. "Well, as I was saying, I saw Mr. Numble. He'd just received a 'mysterious' note, although neither of us is mystified. The whole thing has all the earmarks of Terez Leland's handiwork. We still have definite recollections of her style. Quite a girl, your sister. Lots of spunk."

"Terez?" I gasp. "What's she writing to Bumble about?"

Shrink corrects my 'Bumble' with a twinkle in her eye: "Mr. *Numble* now knows that a certain Frank Flatsam—the resident problem I was about to mention before—is responsible for an increasing number of rather major misdemeanors. Not the least of which is your black eye. Mr. Numble had already guessed that a lot could be attributed to Frank; now he has proof."

"But how do you know the note is from Terez?" I ask in disbelief.

"Terez does things with a certain flair. She has her own unmistakable trademark," observes Shrink. "What she doesn't realize is that Mr. Numble remembers her methods very well—and, Michelle, you must promise *not* to tell your sister about this!"

"Oh, sure. I mean, no. I won't say a thing," I promise. "But what's Bumble, er, Mr. Numble going to do now that he has some goods on Frank?"

"He's already done it," Shrink says grandly. "Frank is finished for now. Suspended—for at least three months. And Mr. Numble has also called for a police investigation into Frank's possible involvement with drugs. This suspension could be only the beginning of Frank's woes."

Shrink sips her coffee reflectively. "I've tried time and again to talk to Frank. There's so much turmoil inside him. He's so angry. I thought Bonnie would be good for him, but she wasn't enough, I guess. Now that he's established a reputation, he feels he's got to be a tough." Shrink shakes her head sadly and pours more coffee.

We sit silent for a while. She looks quizzically at me. "But it's not just Frank, is it? You were going to say something else—about learning that appearances don't count. That can be a long and painful lesson to learn, don't you think?"

I nod, and suddenly start to talk about Klutzy. I mean, it all just pours out, and little Shrink takes it all in. I could kick myself for the big, fat tears that roll down my nose, but Shrink doesn't bat an eye. She digs in her track suit pocket and hands me a tissue.

"Thanks," I sniffle, having finally unloaded my story.

"So let's list the major problems you're

facing," Shrink summarizes. "Firstly, you feel you've deserted your best friend, as well as exploiting her talent..."

"Yes," I hiccup. "She must think I'm a back-stabbing double-crosser."

"Let me finish," commands Shrink. "Secondly, you want to tell Tim Winscott the truth without looking like, um, er..."

"Without looking like a total jerk," I finish.

"Yes. Right. Now we've got the picture," and Shrink looks completely satisfied with life.

"*You've* got it," I observe glumly, "but *I've* got to live with it."

"Come now, Michelle," says Shrink. "Things were definitely worse when Frank was on your trail, weren't they?"

"True," I concede.

"Now you just have to come up with a plan of action to get things back the way you want them."

"True again." But I still feel dubious.

Shrink pours us more coffee and pulls some chocolate chip cookies out of the dissecting cupboard. She pats my arm.

"Tell me, how would you like things to work out for you and Dora?" she asks innocently, as if it's the easiest question ever.

When I stare back blankly, she adds, "You know, in your ideal world—tell me, very simply, what would make you happy?"

"Uh, well," I struggle, trying to think of heaven somewhere up beyond the endless sky. "I guess I'd like to give Klutzy back the 'Peanut Butter' poem—you know, let *her* get the credit—and, gee, I don't know..."

"You want to get things straight between you and Dora. You want her to see you as a friend of good faith."

"Yes," I confirm. "I want her to know I'm the same as always." I think for a second. "I want..."

"Yes?" encourages Shrink.

"I want to be friends again, no matter what anyone says." The realization grows in me. "That's something I'm sure about now," I say firmly.

"What about Tim Winscott?" asks Shrink. "What will he say when he finds you're not what he thought? After all, he badly needs a poetry columnist just now. I heard the principal at Alexander Henry and Mr. Numble talking to him rather seriously about the subject."

"So the pressure is on Tim—he really needs that column?" I ask, an idea taking form in my brain.

Shrink nods, "That's right. I believe Mr. Numble even set a deadline. He really wants the intellectual quality of the school paper raised. Says there has to be something to balance all those sports reports and social notes."

I start adding up what Shrink has just told me. She doesn't interrupt my calculations. I finally grin. "I guess Tim Winscott's ideal world would include a terrific poetry columnist."

"Uh huh," smiles Shrink as I bounce down from my lab stool.

"See you, Mrs. Small. I've got a few visits to make." I feel like skipping out of the lab. My life is beginning to smell like roses.

Chapter Twelve

THE PLAN

I'M STANDING outside the basement 'rabbit warren' that passes for the *Herald* office over at Alexander Henry Senior High. "Er, excuse me, is Tim in?" I call again to the glamorous girl hammering away at the typewriter.

I've been standing at the counter for a good two minutes. I'm nervous enough—without a difficult female ignoring me and making life harder.

Glamor Girl yanks at the paper she's working on, and efficiently flips in another sheet. She peers through black mascara-ed eyelashes: "Oh, you been there long?"

"Only about five hours," I say casually. "I'm supposed to meet Tim Winscott here."

She points to a half open door. "Sure, he's in there."

Then Tim appears from the inside office. "Hi, Michelle. Did you meet Gina, our star typist?"

At this, Gina melts like a puddle of liquid type-eraser. I get the picture.

Tim smiles at me. "Come on in. I'll show you your poem ready to go to press."

Gina pops her bubble gum. "Good writing, kid. Keep it up. You could be a real asset around here."

I flash her a sick grin and follow Tim into the printing room.

"Tim, I want to get something straight right away," I blurt out.

"Sure, what's that?"

"Now, you like the poem, right?"

"Right."

"And you want the writer of that poem to take over the poetry column, right?"

"Right again. You planning to go into law, Michelle? You sound like Perry Mason ready to call in the jury."

"Actually, I *am* going to call someone in. But first I want your promise on that columnist's job."

Tim looks at me hard, trying to figure out what I'm getting at. "Well, Michelle, there's just one condition. I need to see more of your writing so I can tell if it's as good as the piece on Mildew's bulletin board..."

I cut Tim off. "Oh, there's plenty more good stuff where that came from. I guarantee it."

Tim smiles at my assurance. "Then I guarantee the job."

"OK, wait here!" I make a mad dash out of the printing room. Gina looks up, surprised, and pops another bubble.

I open the *Herald* office door, praying that Klutzy is still waiting in the hall.

"Now, Klutz," I say urgently. "Follow me."

Gina gawks at Klutzy. I make the intros: "Gina, this is Klutzy, er, Dora Klutzmann. Klutz, Gina."

I take Klutz into the printing room, where Tim is patiently waiting. "Uh, Tim, meet the author of 'Peanut Butter Is Forever,'" I say nervously. "This is Dora Klutzmann, your new poetry columnist."

Klutz gives Tim a weak smile. I can see that her reaction to him is like mine first was—weak in the knees.

"Uh, hi, er, Dora," says Tim, looking confused.

"Oh, just call me Klutzy," she squeaks.

"And *my* friends call me Mitch, not Michelle," I say, feeling as if I want to be in on the action.

"Okay, Mitch," laughs Tim. He sits down as if he can't quite take the shock. "You two have got me baffled. Explain, please."

Between us, Klutz and I stumble out the story. Or some of it at least. Tim studies his Adidas as we finish talking. There's a nice kind of thinking crinkle in his forehead.

"Klutzy," he says, "I want to see more of your writing before we finalize this. But for now I'll take Mitch's word on your ability, and give you the poetry column job. It won't be all your own writing anyway. You'll have to get to know other outstanding writers around both the junior and senior high school, and use their stuff, too."

"I'll try," says Klutzy, dubiously. "But like we kind of told you just now, I have trouble getting to know people."

"I'll help you with that," says Tim firmly.

I've never seen Klutzy uncloud so quickly. She looks all shining and hopeful—almost pretty, even. "I'd love the job," she says sincerely.

Then Tim turns his gorgeous, smoldering gray eyes on me: "And *you*, Mitch, are in trouble. What you've done is called plagiarism."

I sigh. "So what else is new? I'm always in trouble these days."

Tim keeps his tough look. "I think Klutzy will agree with me on this: we won't say a thing to anyone...if you'll work with us on the *Herald*." He grins. "Like I told you, I could use a junior editor."

I gasp: "Me? A junior editor! You must be joking!"

"I like divergent thinkers, Mitch," says Tim. "And my guess is that you're one of them. Do you want the job or not?"

"Oh, *yes*, of course!" I nearly shout. "What do I do as a junior editor?"

"Empty garbage cans, run errands... things like that," grins Tim disarmingly. "But before you start, let's you two and Gina and I go have a cola to celebrate."

Chapter Thirteen

PEANUT BUTTER IS FOREVER

"HI YA, Klutz. How's the paper chase?" I yell as I come into the *Herald* office.

"OK," she says without even bothering to look up from her typing.

"Klutz, you work like a dog in here," I complain. "Take a break!"

"Tim needs this typing done, and Gina is busy," she answers. There's an edge to her voice.

"Funny how Gina is *always* busy when you're around. If you ask me, Tim and Gina are *using* you."

"Nobody's asking you," Klutzy snaps.

The typewriter chops brokenly at the silence between us.

"Hey, Klutzy," I begin softly, "You don't have to get all upset..."

"I'm not upset," she almost shouts. "I have a typing deadline, that's all."

"All right, all right!" and I turn to tidy up a few papers. My junior editor's job, I find, is training me for a stunning career as a janitor!

I'm willing to forget a bad beginning to a conversation, but Klutzy can't leave bad enough alone.

"And Tim doesn't want anyone calling me Klutzy any more," she adds. "From now on, I'm Dora."

I can't believe my ears. "You expect *me* to call you Dora? After all these years? You tell Tim Winscott to go chase himself! As a matter of fact, I'll tell him so myself."

"Tim is trying to help me with a new image," says Dora primly. "And besides, you seem to forget all the years pretty easily when it's convenient."

Hitting below the belt. I try to be calm, reasonable. "Klutzy, you *know* I was told I couldn't be buddies with you."

"I said not to call me Klutzy!"

"All right! Dora, then," I sigh. "You know that I couldn't help what happened."

"I'd like to know where your parents suddenly got a bad opinion of me, that's all."

"They didn't *suddenly* get a bad opinion of you..." I bluster.

"Oh! So they *always* had a bad opinion?!" Competing with Klutzy's logic is a losing battle.

"No!" I moan, "No, it's just that they thought we should branch out in our friendships..."

"You didn't just branch out, Mitch. You cut the whole tree down!"

"Oh, Klutzy, c'mon..."

"DON'T 'Oh, Klutzy' me!" Klutz rages.

I pound my forehead with my fist, hoping it'll help me to remember the name *Dora*.

"That stupid Tim," I hiss. "Him and his big ideas."

Klutzy turns a light shade of purple. "Tim just happens to be one of my few friends in the whole world. So don't call him stupid. He's heard the whole story, Mitch, and I know he thinks you've been pretty rotten in all this."

Now it's my turn to get mad. "I get it! It's *Tim* who's filled your head with all these ideas against me."

"Tim hasn't filled my head with anything. We've talked, that's all."

"You didn't use to accuse me of being

a rotten friend. That's only happened since you and Tim have had your little talks."

Klutzy's stare could make icicles. Her voice is frozen. "I didn't *use* to because all this hadn't happened then. Things have changed."

I remain the hopeless optimist. "Things haven't changed! Now that I've got a legitimate excuse to see you—which is this *Herald* job—we'll just go back to being friends again. My family won't know the difference."

Klutzy starts thumping the typewriter. Only this time, she uses the one-finger hammer method. It's as if she's pounding out all her frustrations—one letter at a time.

I decide to try once more. "C'mon, Klutz. What d'ya say? Can't we just go back to being the same old buddies we've always been?"

Klutzy at least stops typing. She looks at me coldly. "You just don't get it, do you, Mitch? We can *never* be the same friends we were."

I stare in disbelief. I search Klutzy's face for any sign of humor—is this a joke? But Klutzy is dead serious. This is no little spat, either. She means every word.

"You're saying that's *it*? No more Klutzy and Mitch?" I say weakly.

Klutzy softens a little with pity. "I've been wanting to settle things with you, Mitch. And instead of facing up to you, I've just been acting witchy lately. Now I'm glad it's out."

She looks down. I notice she's wearing nail polish. A soft plum color. That's not the Klutzy I used to know. She'd never have thought of using nail polish before. I now see she's done something to her hair, too. It's all fluffy and soft around her face.

Klutzy glances back up. She seems a little concerned about me at least. "Don't you see, Mitch?" she asks. "We were kids who trusted each other. And then you just took off, right when I needed you most. You changed a little in that time. And I changed a lot. I've changed even more since meeting Tim—and Gina, of course. Things change, that's all."

We let the silence speak for a minute.

I know what Klutzy is talking about. There isn't much more to be said.

I make an attempt at a smile. "Only

peanut butter is forever, right?"

Klutzy chokes out a laugh, "Yeah, right."

We both stare down at the floor. It's as if we're in some kind of unreal television ad for 'Wonder Floor Polish.'

I cough to get my mouth working again. "Well, bye, Klutz. See you around, I guess."

"Good-bye, Mitch."

I walk down the school steps and trudge off home. I think of the old game, 'How do you get peanut butter off the roof of your mouth?'

And how do you get a huge lump of hurt out of your throat when everything goes wrong? I swallow hard but the lump is still there.

If I've learned anything from Mama, I've learned the value of citing at least one useless slogan a day. Terez says that Mama's philosophy of life is: 'A proverb a day keeps the grieves away.'

So, for now, I choose 'Time heals all wounds.' It sounds like something Mama or Terez would throw my way at a time like this.

It'll do for now—to keep me from considering suicide.

I can just see the giant headlines: "GIRL OVERDOSES ON PEANUT BUTTER"! But with *my* luck, Klutzy wouldn't even notice the newspaper that day.

Chapter Fourteen

ON MY WAY

A T HOME I slam doors behind me and head for my bedroom.

"Hey, Bonzo," Terez comes yelling into my room. "Do you have to go around smashing all the doors? You could make an effort to develop a little finesse—you know..." She begins flitting about like Tinker Bell and speaking like an English school marm: "O—pen and cl—ose each door del—i—cate—ly and th—ink a—bout walk—ing gr—ace—ful—ly."

I let my books slam down on the floor. "Go stuff it, Terez."

Her pencilled eyebrows fly up, ready for battle. Then she peers closely at me.

"What's wrong with you, Mitch? You look like something right out of 'World of the Living Dead.'"

"Wrong with me?" I fume. "Klutzy has turned the tables and rejected me. Bonnie thinks I'm a flake. All of Frank's crowd think I'm a stoolie and a wimp. And Tim Winscott thinks I'm no more than a resident dishrag at the *Herald*. Nothing's wrong. Life is beautiful."

Terez lounges down at the end of my bed. "So poor old Mitch is a social reject. What d'you want me to do about it?"

Terez is remarkable. She has the knack of brilliantly summarizing misery.

"What can you do? Just get out of my room, that's all," I huff. "I'd rather be a social reject than a social climber like some people around this house."

Terez chooses to ignore my ranting. She's already examining her toenail polish—a sure sign that she's thinking through a problem.

"Let's see now," she muses aloud. "Mama spent a few thousand on braces so your teeth aren't crooked; you don't have bad breath—except maybe after a pepperoni pizza; and you're always using *my* deodorant, so you can't have B.O. You shower every morning, right? And you don't pick your nose..."

"OUT, Terez!" I yell.

"You made friends before this, so you must have *some* social skills," she continues to analyze. "You dress well enough.

Not like me, of course, but your jeans are
a decent cut. You have a fantastic smile
and gorgeous eyes. Your hair looks
great."

I sit up, listening. "I do? It does?"

Terez goes on. "But a little make-up would do wonders, and your eyebrows could stand a good plucking..."

"No way!" I slump down on my pillow again.

"...but even though you're as natural as plain yogurt, all my friends say you're cute, and a really neat person."

"They do?" I gasp.

Terez stretches like a cat. She checks her hair in my big mirror and begins her slinky walk out of my room. "Any time you want a tune-up, just say the word. But you're a winner, kid. Just you believe it."

Then Terez pulls the door her way. "All you've really got to learn is to close a door like *this*."

Click. Gently. Almost as if it never happened.

Terez doesn't think in analogies. She thinks in Max Factor and Calvin Klein. But she has her way of driving home a point.

Close the door—gently. That's what I need to do with Klutzy and our friendship. Not go madly slamming about. Just close the door quietly behind me and carry on to new things.

"I'm going to take this philosophically," I say firmly to myself.

I look in the mirror to check out what Terez has said. Will anyone ever want to be my friend again? Would you buy a used car from this face?

The nose is the same as in the days when Terez used to call me Noseholes. I try to flatten my nostrils, and consider plastic surgery.

I think about Terez's offer of a tune-up. Nope. Incandescent eyes and purple lips just aren't me.

I stare hard and long into the mirror. I guess I do have some things going for me, as Terez says. I'm not exactly a sex symbol, but I'll pass. I guess I have to be satisfied with myself the way I am.

About an hour later, the phone rings.

"Hello, Mitch. This is Dora," says a familiar voice.

"Dora?" I ask, surprised.

"Yes, Klutzmann. You know..." she says impatiently.

"Sure; of course. Uh, hi, Dora," I manage.

"Mitch, I started cleaning my old memory box as soon as I got home. I was in the mood to throw a lot of things away."

"I noticed," I say softly.

"Well, I found our class pictures from elementary school. And our 'Little Devils Club' banner—remember, in third grade? And the letters you sent when you were on vacations." Klutzy's voice sounds choked up. "I just can't throw away all the memories—all the good times we've had together, Mitch. I'm phoning to say I was wrong and I hope . . ." she sobs.

"Hey, Klutz," I cut in. "I mean, Dora. There's a good show on at the Ritz. Let's catch the 7:30."

Klutzy sniffles and laughs shakily, "Sounds great, Mitch. See you at the theater door."

I pull on my best jeans and my old Fonz 'Happy Days' T-shirt. "Peanut Butter Is Forever," I think with satisfaction. "But other things in life can be forever, too."

And for the first time in weeks I feel good, as if I've hit the real truth.

As I run downstairs, Mama smiles back my smile. "You look more chipper now, love," she says. "You've been so morose these past weeks, Michelle. I've worried so much about you, and now it's sunshine to see you smile."

Mama gives me a hug. "You're going out, I see. Are you on your way now?"

"I'm on my way all right, in more ways than one," I grin. "And I'm off to meet a friend—a very dear friend."

"Oh, who's that?" Mama questions.

"Dora Klutzmann, alias Klutzy," I say, steeling myself for an onslaught of pleadings and warnings.

Mama looks taken aback. "Do you really think..."

"Yes, I *really* think so, Mama," I say firmly. "Like you always say, 'To thine own friend be true.'"

"You've been *so* miserable without her," Mama sighs. "And Dora *has* changed so much lately, from what I've heard. Mrs. Friedman told me—oh, do you remember the Klutzmanns' neighbor who goes to aerobics class with me? Well, Madge Friedman says that Dora has some school newspaper job that is quite prestigious, and it's given Dora a whole new lease on life."

I add dryly: "And now Mrs. Friedman's daughter, Lynn, will actually speak to Dora."

"Yes!" says Mama, full of enthusiasm. "Isn't it wonderful how things change!"

I resist a smirk. "It's truly incredible, Mama. And since Dora is obviously getting it together, how about lifting the ban on the Klutzmanns?"

Mama wears her 'convenor-at-the-United-Nations' look. She's about to set forth policy that will solve the world's problems: "You can see Dora, I suppose, since you're so set on it—but don't go around her home. That father and his..."

"Yes, Mama, I know. But it's Dora who's my friend, remember. I'm not out to adopt her family."

Mama sighs again. "I guess you know what you're doing. Have a good time, then, and be in by eleven."

I'm astounded that it's been so easy. "Thanks, Mama," I whisper.

"Oh, and Mitch," Mama finishes, "The expression is: 'To thine own *self* be true.'"

"Yep. I'm gonna' do *that* too," I laugh.

I open the door, and am truly on my way.

And the peace deep inside me feels like it is, and will remain, always and forever.

About the Author

Melanie Zola was born in Calgary and raised in Lethbridge, Alberta. She now lives in Vancouver with her husband (also a writer) and her five-year-old daughter. Melanie is a teacher who spends the summer holidays writing. *Peanut Butter Is Forever* is her first novel.

Titles in the Series

Printed in U.S.A.